SURVIVOR STORIES™

TERRORIST ATTACK

True Stories of Survival

Jennifer Silate

rosen publishing's
rosen central

New York

Published in 2007 by The Rosen Publishing Group, Inc.
29 East 21st Street, New York, NY 10010

First Edition

Library of Congress Cataloging-in-Publication Data

Silate, Jennifer.
Terrorist attack : true stories of survival / Jennifer Silate. – 1st ed.
p. cm. – (Survivor stories)
Includes bibliographical references and index.
ISBN-13: 978-1-4042-1001-1
ISBN-10: 1-4042-1001-6 (library binding)
1. Victims of terrorism–Juvenile literature. 2. Terrorism–Juvenile literature.
I. Title.
HV6431.S473 2007
363.325–dc22

                                                    2006023342

Printed in China

On the cover: New Yorkers run from the World Trade Center as one of the towers collapses after being hit by an airplane on September 11, 2001.

CONTENTS

Terrorist attacks strike all over the world. Here, rescuers carry an injured man from the scene of an attack that killed six people in Baghdad, Iraq, on November 18, 2005.

INTRODUCTION

Terrorist attacks have happened throughout history. Most early terrorist organizations fought primarily against governments by murdering key officials. In 1914, a Serbian terrorist killed Archduke Franz Ferdinand, the man who was to be king of Austria-Hungry. This murder was the event that started World War I.

In the 1950s and 1960s, the nature of terrorism changed. After World War II, more and more terrorist organizations began forming throughout the world. Many of these organizations opposed the governments running their countries and went to extreme lengths to show their disapproval. Terrorists attacked local authorities, hijacked planes, and bombed buildings. Many more civilians were killed as a result of these attacks. In places where wars were being fought, terrorist groups often killed civilians as revenge for other deaths in the wars. Terrorists also killed citizens to get a reaction from those they opposed and to spread fear among civilians in an attempt to force governments to give in to their demands.

Today, terrorism is widely defined as the use of violent acts to spread fear in a population in order to pressure public officials or the governments of other countries into taking certain actions. Although widely condemned by governments and large segments of the population, terrorists are viewed as heroes or freedom fighters by those who agree with their goals. Many countries disagree over which groups in the world should be considered terrorists. In places where rulers are accused of violating human rights, those who fight against them may be thought of as terrorists only by the rulers they oppose. Most groups who spread fear by committing acts of violence, often targeting civilians, are considered terrorists.

Terrorists can be found all over the world. Some organizations, like Al Qaeda, are very large, with smaller groups of members located in many different countries. Some terrorists act alone or with only a few other like-minded people. Whether carried out by a large, well-organized group or by a lone attacker, a single act of terror can kill or injure hundreds and even thousands of people.

Thousands of civilians are victims of terrorist attacks each year. Some terrorists kill not only people who they do not agree with politically, but also those who don't share their religious beliefs. Terrorist attacks are often committed with the hopes that the country attacked will wage war or act in such a way as to turn more people against it and what it stands for. Terrorists believe that their actions are justified to bring about the changes they feel are necessary.

Acts of terror often bring about extreme pain and suffering. These acts also have inspired extreme kindness and courage within the targeted population. Those attacked often risk their own lives to save the lives of others. In the aftermath of a terrorist attack, there are numerous examples of people who triumph over fear and anger to rebuild their lives and help those who have also suffered. There are thousands of inspiring stories from terror survivors all over the world. These stories reveal how individuals and society as a whole can overcome the worst in human nature to uncover the best.

1

THE OKLAHOMA CITY BOMBING

On April 19, 1995, at 9:02 AM, a rental truck blew up outside the Alfred P. Murrah Federal Building in Oklahoma City, Oklahoma. The truck was filled with 5,000 pounds of explosive material. In an instant, the lives of thousands of people changed forever.

THE SHOCK AFTER THE BOMB

Within two hours of the bombing, police arrested a man named Timothy McVeigh. McVeigh had been pulled over for driving without license plates on his car. The officer who stopped him saw a gun hidden in his jacket. In time, the United States would find out that McVeigh was responsible for what was then the worst terrorist attack to ever take place in America. People were stunned to find out that the person behind this attack was not only a U.S. citizen, but also a war veteran. McVeigh worked with another man, Terry Nichols, to plan the bombing. McVeigh, however, drove the truck and set off the explosives inside it.

Timothy McVeigh's bomb left a hole nine stories high in the Alfred P. Murrah Federal Building in Oklahoma City, Oklahoma. The effect of the blast was felt as far as thirty miles away.

In the years to follow, McVeigh admitted that he bombed the Alfred P. Murrah Federal Building to avenge the deaths of eighty members of the Branch Davidians, a religious group, who died in an inferno after a standoff with federal agents in Waco, Texas, in 1993. In McVeigh's view, these people were murdered by the federal government. He executed the Oklahoma City bombing exactly two years after the events in Waco.

SEARCHING FOR SURVIVORS

The impact of the blast from the terrorist attack ripped the front off the building and damaged hundreds of others in the area. The Murrah Building was home to local offices for several different federal agencies and a day-care center. One hundred and sixty-eight people died as a result of the bombing. Of those people, nineteen were children who had been in the day-care center located in the front of the building. Hundreds of people who lived nearby were left without homes. Thousands of people were without jobs.

More than 12,000 people helped with the search-and-rescue and relief operation. Many people were trapped under large, heavy pieces of concrete that had once been the walls of the building. Rescuers and their search-and-rescue dogs worked tirelessly for more than two weeks to find survivors.

Some experts estimate that one-third of the population in Oklahoma City, more than 380,000 people, knew someone who was killed or injured. More than 1,000 people survived the terrible blast. Of those survivors, there are many amazing stories of heroism and courage.

Daina Bradley

Daina Bradley entered the Murrah Building some time after 8 AM on April 19, 1995. She was going to the Social Security office with her

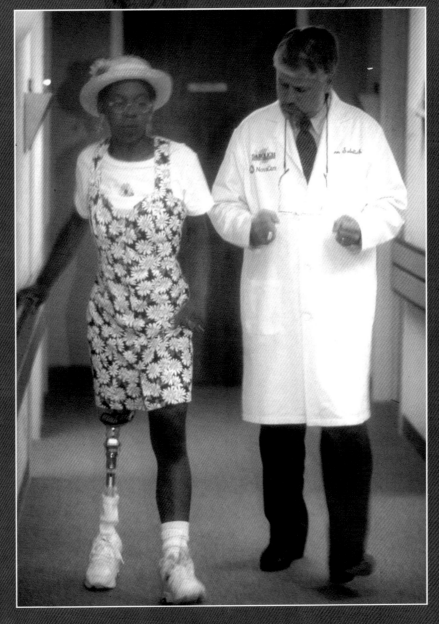

Emergency workers had to cut off Daina Bradley's right leg to rescue her from the scene of the Oklahoma City bombing. With time and patience, she has learned to walk with an artificial leg.

mother, sister, son, and daughter. While Bradley waited in line to be helped, she saw a yellow moving truck pull up outside of the building. She saw someone exit the truck and move quickly away. Bradley thought that it seemed odd. In a moment, there was a flash and Bradley was alone, trapped under debris. She could hear her mother, daughter, and son, but she could not get to them. The damaged building moved, and she could no longer hear them. Bradley feared that they had died. She worried that she would not make it out alive either.

When rescue workers found her, they realized that the only way that Bradley could be removed from the rubble was to cut off her leg. She told them to do what was necessary to save her. The rescue workers were able to cut off her leg safely and take her to the hospital. She would survive.

REBECCA AND BRANDON DENNY

Only six children survived the bombing. Among them were two-year-old Rebecca Denny and three-year-old Brandon Denny. The brother and sister were in the America's Kids day-care center on the second floor of the Murrah Building. The day-care center was almost directly above where Timothy McVeigh parked his rented truck filled with explosives. The truck was less than 60 feet (18 meters) away.

At the time of the explosion, the Denny children were likely near the front of the building. The force of the explosion threw them across the day-care center to the other side of the building. Rubble tumbled on top of the children. Glass, concrete, and other debris flew at them with tremendous force. Rescue workers rushed to the area where the children were believed to have been. Rebecca and Brandon were found and rushed to the hospital.

Rebecca and Brandon's parents, Jim and Claudia Denny, had no idea if their children had survived. They rushed from their jobs to the bombsite. When they saw the hole left by the bomb where the day care had once been, they prepared for the worst. They heard on the news

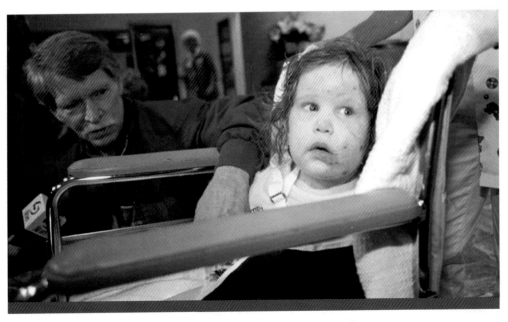

Rebecca Denny is comforted by her father after undergoing treatment for her injuries from the Oklahoma City bombing. She and her brother, Brandon, were two of only six children to survive the blast.

that a girl fitting Rebecca's description was in a local hospital later that morning. To their amazement, it was their daughter. She was badly cut and bruised. Around 4 PM, they received word that Brandon was also alive, though terribly injured. Doctors were unsure if he would live or die.

Rebecca was in the hospital for ten days and had three surgeries. Brandon, however, was in the hospital for more than seventy days. His recovery has been difficult. He has had five brain surgeries to remove the debris in his skull and to repair injuries. He walks with a limp, has seizures, and cannot use his right hand well. Despite these injuries, both children have made remarkable recoveries. There are only a few scars left on Rebecca's face from where she was cut during the bombing. Brandon still has to go to therapy, but he's getting better and is not about to give up.

HEALING AFTER TERROR

For most survivors, including Daina Bradley and the Denny children, healing has not just been about physical injuries. Memories of those left behind and of the events of the Oklahoma City bombing have left many people emotionally scarred. Bradley had nightmares and was depressed after the bombing. Her sister, Felicia, survived, but was badly burned. As Daina had feared, her children and mother died. She was devastated. She has even felt guilty for having taken them with her that day. In time, life has gotten a little easier. Bradley got married

The Oklahoma City National Memorial, which stands on the site of the bombing, includes a field of chairs *(foreground)*, one for each person killed; a museum *(background)*; and the Survivor Tree *(in front of the museum, to the right)*.

and had another child. She was even able to walk down the aisle during her wedding with the help of an artificial leg.

The Denny children do not remember much of the bombing. They have, however, taken part in the memorial ceremonies held at the site of the bombing with the other surviving children. The memorial features 168 chairs to remember those who died and a wall listing all of the survivors. Overlooking the memorial is a tree that withstood the impact of the explosion. It is called the Survivor Tree. The Survivor Tree serves as a reminder that life goes on even after incredible pain.

2

AL QAEDA
STRIKES AMERICA

Al Qaeda is an international Muslim terrorist group started by a man named Osama bin Laden, who issued two fatwas, or declarations of war, against the United States. The fatwas called for the killing of Americans by Muslims in response to the United States' involvement in what bin Laden considered Muslim lands, in particular Iraq and Israel. On September 11, 2001, bin Laden's fatwa reached a new level as his supporters carried out one of the worst terrorist attacks in history.

It was clear and sunny along the East Coast on that fateful day. Millions of people headed to work in New York City and Arlington, Virginia, not knowing that they would soon be under attack. At 8:46 AM, Al Qaeda operatives flew a hijacked plane loaded with 10,000 gallons of jet fuel into the North Tower of the World Trade Center in New York City. The impact created a large firebomb. All of the people onboard the plane and an unknown number of people in the building were killed. At 9:03 AM, a second hijacked plane was flown into the South Tower of the World Trade Center. Many people died instantly.

Authorities got word that a flight had also been hijacked around 9:16 AM. But it was too late. At 9:37 AM, Flight 77 crashed at full speed into the Pentagon. All those onboard were killed, as well as many in the building that morning.

A fourth plane, flying from Newark, New Jersey, was hijacked at 9:28 AM by the Al Qaeda terrorists. Many passengers on this plane called their family and loved ones when they realized what was happening. The passengers worked together to fight the terrorists. Their fighting forced the terrorists to crash the plane in a field in Pennsylvania. Officials believe that the intended target was the White House or Capitol building. The actions of the passengers onboard saved countless lives.

The grizzly image of the twin towers being attacked shocked people all over the world.

Meanwhile, back in New York, the situation was getting worse. At 9:59 AM, the South Tower collapsed, sending tons of dust and debris into the streets and damaging nearby buildings. Twenty-nine minutes later, the North Tower fell.

More than 3,000 people died as a result of the attacks of September 11. Hundreds of thousands were affected. The many people who made it out of the World Trade Center towers and the Pentagon building that day still live with the memories of the terrorist attacks. For most, their lives have been changed forever.

CLAIRE MCINTYRE

Claire McIntyre worked on the ninety-first floor of the North Tower of

Quick thinking and fast action after the planes hit the North Tower saved the lives of Claire McIntyre and her coworkers.

the World Trade Center for the American Bureau of Shipping. In the seconds before the first plane smashed into the building, just three floors above her office, she heard the loud roar of a jet plane and saw a wing and part of its body. Moments later, the building started to sway from the shock of the impact. McIntyre and her ten coworkers knew they had to get out of the building. They rushed to the nearest stairwell and saw that water from sprinklers was flooding the stairs. Sheetrock, the material used to build walls, was blocking the stairs above them. The 1,344 people above the ninety-first floor were trapped. No one would survive.

McIntyre and her coworkers began the long walk down the stairs. Thick, black smoke filled the air. They joined thousands of others who were also fleeing the building. One hour later, McIntyre and her coworkers were on the street. Within minutes, the South Tower gave way and fell. Claire McIntyre once again had to find safety. She was one of the lucky ones: she survived.

BRIAN CLARK

Brian Clark worked for Euro Brokers on the eighty-fourth floor of the World Trade Center's South Tower. He was in his office the morning of September 11, 2001. When the first plane hit the North Tower, the lights dimmed and flames filled the view from his office window. He was a fire warden for his floor and had a whistle and flashlight. He grabbed these items and screamed for everyone to leave the office. However, the people in the South Tower were instructed to stay inside. They were told that they were safe. Everyone in the office was in shock and concerned about what was going on in the North Tower.

When the second plane smashed into the South Tower, it struck about five floors below where Clark was working. The walls twisted, the ceiling crumbled, the lights went out, and the building swayed violently. The floor filled with black smoke and dust. Clark started heading down the stairwell with several other people. They encountered very thick smoke a few floors down and a woman they were with suggested that they go up toward the roof. She thought that they could be rescued by helicopter there. Clark, however, heard someone calling for help and decided to check it out. It was a man named Stanley Praimnath. He was trapped in his office on the eighty-first floor by a piece of metal from the plane.

Clark and Ronald DiFrancesco left their coworkers to help him. The air was thick with dust and only Clark could breathe well enough to find and help the man. When he found the trapped man, he helped him move the debris that had fallen. Clark pulled Praimnath up over the remaining debris to help him escape his office.

The two men decided to try to go down the stairs to find safety. They made their way through the smoke and debris down the eighty-one flights of stairs. On their way down, they came across many people. Some were injured; some were going back up the stairs to help those on the higher floors. The men even stopped in a conference room to phone their wives to tell them that they were all right. In time, the men made it to the ground floor. As they were leaving the building, a police officer warned them of falling debris. They made a run for it.

The two men had been out of the building for only about five minutes when the South Tower fell. They ran from the church where they had sought shelter away from the wave of dust that was quickly filling the air. In time, Clark made it to the piers on the east side of Manhattan and was able to get on a ferry across the Hudson River to Jersey City, New Jersey. As he rode the ferry home, he looked at the city and saw that the North Tower had also fallen. What he did not know was that he had been one of only four people above the eightieth floor in the South Tower that day to survive.

APRIL AND ELISHA GALLOP

September 11, 2001, was April Gallop's first day back at work in the Pentagon after having her son, Elisha. She was at her desk, turning on her computer, with two-month-old Elisha in a stroller nearby. Suddenly, she heard a horrible noise, and a large explosion sent her flying across the office. American Airlines Flight 77 had just crashed into the side of the Pentagon. April lost consciousness.

When she awoke, the air was filled with black smoke and she could hear Elisha crying. He was buried under debris. April pulled Elisha from the rubble and struggled to get him out of the building.

Along the way, April stopped to help whomever she could. When she was able to finally escape the burning building, she fainted. A man passing by picked up Elisha and helped to get him and April to the hospital for care. The mother and child would survive, but their troubles were just beginning.

April Gallop addresses a news conference concerning driver's licenses for illegal aliens. She shows a picture of her son being taken from the Pentagon on September 11.

SURVIVORS OF SEPTEMBER 11

In the months and years to follow, the effects of the terrorist attacks on September 11 have become well known. Many people suffered from not only physical pain, but also emotional pain. Claire McIntyre and Brian Clark have each gone back to work for their former companies. They lost many friends and coworkers, and each attended group counseling sessions to help them deal with their grief. McIntyre says she feels that she needs to make the most of the life she has when so many others lost theirs. Clark went back to work eight days after the attack, though he says that for a time he felt unable to focus on his work.

Life has not been easy since the attacks for April and Elisha Gallop. April's spine was injured in the attack on the Pentagon, and she still experiences pain. Elisha had some hearing loss and was slower to learn to walk and run than other children. Sometimes, when April hears Elisha cry or smells fuel, she has flashbacks to the terror she experienced on September 11. She has started a company that works to get funds for other survivors, veterans, and their children. She hopes that her work will help make their lives and her own a little bit easier.

The USS Cole

Al Qaeda has attacked Americans outside of the United States, too. On October 12, 2000, a small boat crashed into the USS Cole while it was refueling at a dock in Aden, Yemen, a country on the Arabian Peninsula. The small boat was carrying powerful explosives. The explosion tore a 40-by-60 foot (12-by-18 meter) hole into the side of the 505-foot (154 m) ship, nearly sinking it. In the suicide attack, seventeen sailors were killed and thirty-nine were injured.

Andrew Nemeth was one of the 325-member crew aboard the USS Cole that day. He was getting his lunch when the explosion rocked the boat. Nemeth says that he did not hear the explosion, but

This photograph shows the gaping hole in the USS *Cole* after it was attacked by terrorists on October 12, 2000. Andrew Nemeth (inset) leaves a Yemeni hospital for further treatment in Germany.

he was thrown in the air by its force. He did not know that he had been hurt until a medic stopped to help him. His head was bleeding, and he was taken to a nearby hospital.

Nemeth says he was not comfortable until he was transferred to a U.S. hospital. He said he did not know whom to trust after the bombing in Yemen. Despite his injuries and the loss of some good friends, Nemeth hoped to get back out to sea, saying that if he let the bombing stop him from returning to duty, the terrorists win.

3
TERROR ATTACKS IN EUROPE

The United States is not the only target for Al Qaeda terrorist acts. In 2003, the United States and several other countries, including Spain and Britain, invaded Iraq. They wanted to remove Saddam Hussein, Iraq's dictator, from power. The countries thought that Hussein was dangerous to his people and others around the world. In October 2003, Osama bin Laden warned that countries helping the United States in Iraq would become targets of Al Qaeda violence.

MADRID IN MARCH

On Friday, March 11, 2004, thousands of people packed into the commuter trains in Madrid, Spain. Many were on their way to work or school. Ten bombs were also on four of those trains. Moroccan terrorists tied to Al Qaeda had put 22 pounds (10 kg) of explosives in backpacks. At 7:39 AM, the terrorists used cell phones to explode several bombs placed on two trains. One train was in the Atocha Station in Madrid; the other was nearing the station. In the next three minutes, several more bombs exploded on two other trains. In all, 191 people died as a result of the bombings. More than 1,500 were injured. The survivors are still overcoming pain and fear in the aftermath of these bombings.

JESUS RAMIREZ

On the morning of March 11, 2004, Jesus Ramirez boarded the train as usual on his way to work. As he looked for a seat, one of the bombs exploded. Ramirez did not know what had happened. Several minutes later, a second bomb exploded. He remembers emergency workers asking him his phone number and then nothing.

After the bombings, Jesus Ramirez became a representative of the Association for the Victims of March 11. He works to help other survivors.

Ramirez was taken to a hospital. He was badly injured and remained unconscious for ten days. Metal and glass from the explosion were lodged throughout his body. His legs were horribly burned. For fifteen days after the bombing, doctors were unsure whether Ramirez would live or die from his injuries.

For Ramirez, recovery has been a slow, painful process. He has to have physical therapy for the injuries that he suffered in the Madrid bombing. He was so emotionally scarred by the experience that it took him two years to even go back to the train station where he once went daily. He worries that even with greater security, it would still be too easy for bombs to be taken aboard a train. Though Ramirez is fearful of another attack, he still thinks that terrorists gain if people do not continue to live freely. He wonders what the terrorists accomplished by their bombing of his and three other trains. Whose life is better because of it?

LONDON BOMBINGS

On July 7, 2005, terrorists bombed public transportation in London, England, as they had in Madrid. Public buses and London Underground (subway) trains were targeted in this attack. At 8:50 AM, three bombs exploded in trains filled with passengers. About an hour later, a bomb went off on a double-decker bus. The bombs killed fifty-two people and injured more than 700 others. London investigators believe that even though the attackers appear to have been inspired by Al Qaeda, they were not directly linked. This view is based in part on the fact that the attackers were all British citizens, born to Muslim immigrants. However, Al Qaeda has since released a videotape that shows footage of one of the attackers. The terrorist organization has also said the attack was in response to Britain's involvement in the war in Iraq. The hunt for terrorists gets more difficult as people outside of terrorist organizations join in their fight.

GILL HICKS

Gill Hicks entered King's Cross Station in London a little before 8:50 AM on July 7, 2005. She was late for work. A man pushed ahead of her onto the first train in the station, and she was unable to board. When the next train arrived, Hicks boarded. Suicide bomber Germaine Lindsey was on that train. He carried powerful explosives in his backpack.

As the train left the station, Lindsey set off the bomb he was carrying. Hicks felt like she could not breathe. The lights went out in the train, and people screamed in the darkness. Hicks suddenly realized that she was on the floor of the train. The emergency lights in the tunnel where the train had stopped were lit. In the dim light, Hicks could see her body. Her feet had almost been entirely severed from her legs. Her legs were also horribly injured. She cried out for someone to help her up from the ground. Another passenger helped to get her up to the bench.

Hicks knew that she was losing a lot of blood. She wrapped the scarf she had worn that day around her legs to try to stop the bleeding. As she fought to stay conscious, Hicks lifted her injured legs up onto the armrests of the bench to help slow the bleeding. Though she desperately wanted to shut her eyes and sleep, she felt she might never wake up if she did.

Rescue workers struggled to get through the smoke filling the long tunnel where Hicks's train had stopped. Through the thickening black smoke, Hicks saw a flashlight. Two police officers approached her and said, "Priority One," acknowledging her need for immediate care.

The two officers, Steve Bryan and Aaron Debnam, worked to keep Hicks alive. They struggled to carry her out of the tunnel and

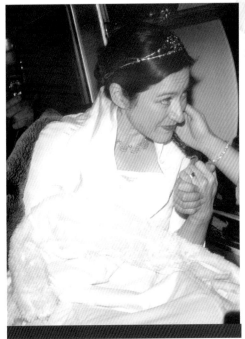

Gill Hicks's dreams came true when she walked down the aisle at her wedding, just five months after the bombing took her legs.

keep her injuries from getting worse. In time, the men were able to get Hicks to the medics waiting outside the tunnel. They left her with the medics and returned to the train to help other victims. The officers were later told that Gill had died. It took them more than three months to find out the truth—she had in fact survived.

Hicks does not remember much from the days following the bombing. When she awoke in the hospital, she remembered a nightmarish vision of what had happened to her legs. In her hospital bed,

Hicks asked the nurse if what she remembered was true. The nurse told her that it was, and that her legs had to be amputated.

Hicks has not let the loss of her legs slow her down. From her hospital bed, she swore that she would walk down the aisle at her wedding, which she had been planning before the explosion. She now has to use prosthetic legs to walk, albeit with some difficulty. Nevertheless, she was able to walk down the aisle at her wedding in December 2005. Attending her wedding were the two men she credits with saving her life: Bryan and Debnam.

Though she definitely misses the use of her legs, Hicks says that she is not angry with the suicide bombers who killed and injured so many in London. She explains that she feels sorry for their families who cannot grieve in public for their loved ones and for the young men who took their own lives in such a senseless act. "I view them as victims, and that helps me feel very sad for them," she told the BBC.

4

TERRORISM AROUND THE WORLD

Though Al Qaeda is one of the most famous and dangerous terrorist groups in recent history, it is not the only one. Terrorists can be found in all parts of the world, fighting against many different governments and people.

THE REAL IRA

England has ruled parts of Ireland for hundreds of years. The Irish have fought the British for independence for almost as long. In the 1960s, that fighting took the form of terrorism. The Provisional Irish Republican Army (IRA) started using bombs and other forms of violence to protest England's rule of a section of the country called Northern Ireland. For thirty years, the IRA terrorized England and Northern Ireland. This time came to be known in Ireland as the "Troubles."

A peace agreement was made in 1997 between the Provisional IRA and the Irish and British governments. A group calling itself the Real IRA formed after the peace agreement. It did not agree with the terms of the peace agreement and carried out more terrorist acts despite the declaration of peace.

On August 15, 1998, the Real IRA committed one of the worst acts of terrorism ever in Ireland. Members set off a 500-pound car bomb in the city of Omagh. It was a busy Saturday afternoon, and the market there was filled with people. The police had been tipped off that there was a bomb in the area, but they were not told the

This amateur video shows the scene of chaos that filled the streets of Omagh after a car bomb exploded in the busy market on August 15, 1998. It also shows people helping injured victims.

correct location. They evacuated people from where they thought the bomb was located, but they were wrong. In fact, they had moved people closer to the actual bomb site.

Around 3 PM, the bomb exploded. Twenty-nine people were killed and more than 300 were injured.

KEVIN SKELTON

Among those at the Omagh market that day were Kevin Skelton, his wife, and their three daughters. They were shopping for school uniforms and supplies. Skelton left his family to go into a different shop. He realized that he had not given his wife, Philomena, money to buy the uniforms and turned to leave. As he was leaving, the powerful bomb exploded. The glass of the shop blew out around him. Skelton rushed over to the store where his wife and daughters had been shopping. To his horror, he discovered that his wife had been killed by the blast. He desperately searched for his daughters. He immediately found two of them, but his youngest was missing. It was two hours until he received news about her. She was alive, but in the hospital with severe injuries to her head.

Skelton and his family are still coping with the memory of that day and the loss of a wife and mother. He has since remarried. He says that his daughters told him that Philomena would not have wanted him to sit around being depressed and, in time, he agreed. In the years after the bombing at Omagh, Skelton and the many other survivors have worked to put the tragedy behind them. The pain might have faded, but the memories are still strong.

PALESTINIAN SUICIDE BOMBERS

Palestinians and Israelis have fought over land for more than fifty years. The fight has resulted in war several times. Extremists in Palestine try to drive Israelis out of Palestinian territory, and even out of Israel, by carrying bombs to places where Israelis are gathered. These suicide bombers kill themselves and others in an attempt to win land back for their people. The bombs that suicide bombers use are often filled with nails, screws, and other small pieces of metal so that even those who are not killed by the explosion are severely injured by flying debris. The survivors of these terrorist attacks often have painful injuries that take a long time to heal. The emotional damage that suicide bombers cause is much greater than the physical pain. The terror felt by those who are attacked can last for years.

ELAD WAFA

Elad Wafa came to Israel from Ethiopia when he was seven years old. He was part of a program to bring African Jews to Israel. He and his family walked from Ethiopia to Sudan, where a plane brought them to their destination. The entire journey took nearly a year. Wafa worked in a vegetable stand in Israel. He said it was a dream to be there from his tiny village in Ethiopia.

On May 19, 2002, a Palestinian suicide bomber changed Wafa's life forever. He remembers seeing a man standing about 6 feet (2 meters) from his vegetable stand that afternoon when his cell phone rang. Wafa turned to pick up his phone just as the man exploded his bomb. Wafa tried three times to get up from the ground, but he could not. He looked over at his arm and saw that a large concrete block was lodged in his shoulder. Emergency workers picked him up and put him on a stretcher. He heard his father calling for him, but he could not respond. Then he lost consciousness.

Wafa woke up in the hospital several days later. Nails and other debris from the bomb had pierced his body and cut his spinal cord in his lower back. At first, he could not use his arms or legs. It took him nearly two years to try to stand. Life has not been easy since the bombing. Wafa does not like depending on others, but he is learning to deal with his injuries. He is working toward getting his high school diploma and has plans to join a disabled basketball team. He says he tries to be positive. "Of course, nothing will be the same. My injuries are permanent, and I see the world in a different way—not so bright and white," Wafa told the BBC.

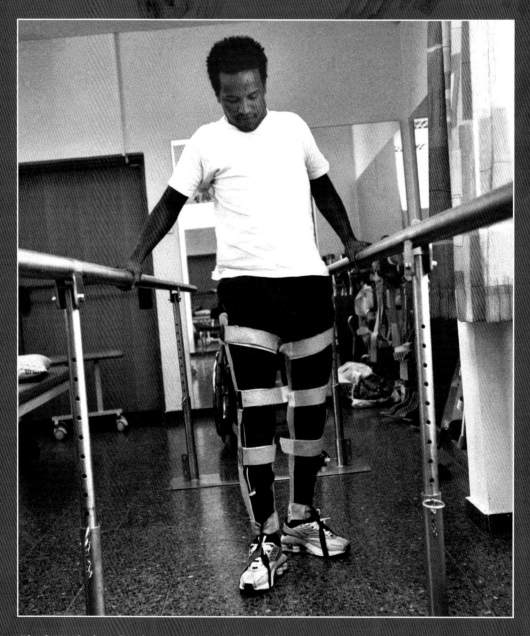

Elad Wafa has had to work very hard to overcome the damage done to his body by a Palestinian suicide bomber. It took him two years to learn how to stand again.

BESLAN, RUSSIA

Another area of the world with constant fighting and terrorist activity is Russia and Chechnya. Chechnya is a republic of Russia. Russia rules Chechnya, but many Chechens wish that this was not so. Some Chechen rebels have resorted to terrorism to protest Russian rule. They have kidnapped many and have bombed public places filled with innocent men, women, and children.

One of the deadliest terrorist attacks by Chechen terrorists happened on September 1, 2004. On that day, they invaded a Beslan school filled with children, teachers, and parents. They took more than 1,000 people hostage. The terrorists grouped the hostages in the gym, placed explosives around them on the floor, and hung bombs from the ceiling and basketball hoops. The hostages were held for three days. Most were not given food or water, or even allowed to go to the restroom or sleep. People who spoke to one another were shot.

On the third day, the Chechen terrorists agreed to let emergency workers come in and get the dead bodies. As the workers approached the school, there was an explosion. The terrorists and the Russian troops, who had been outside the school, started firing at one another. The troops moved in, and the terrorists started shooting the hostages who were fleeing. At least one terrorist blew up a bomb strapped to his body, killing those near him.

GEORGY FARNIYEV

On the third day of the siege at his school, ten-year-old Georgy Farniyev was less than 20 feet (7 meters) away from the first bomb that exploded. Somehow, he escaped with only cuts on his arms and legs, while most of those around him died. After the explosion, Farniyev snuck away to get some water from a broken pipe. As he made his way toward water, another bomb exploded. He returned to the gym to see many people dead and wounded. He decided to hide. Luckily for him, he was found by a Russian soldier during the fighting.

Farniyev was taken to the hospital to have his injuries treated. Meanwhile, his mother was searching frantically for him. She was overjoyed when she received a call from the hospital saying that a boy who looked like her son was there and alive.

More than 340 civilians, including 186 children, died in the Beslan siege, and more than 700 were injured. Many of the survivors were children who will no doubt remember that horrible day and the friends they lost for the rest of their lives.

TERRORISM IN THE FUTURE

Terrorism may not ever end. There will always be people willing to kill for their cause. In 2005, there were 10,000 terrorist attacks and kidnappings worldwide—up from 3,194 in 2004.

Georgy Farniyev holds a picture of himself that was taken during the September 2004 siege at his school in Chechnya. That picture was broadcast around the world to show the terror the children faced.

Hundreds of thousands of lives are changed forever as those affected by terrorist attacks struggle to deal with the pain of injury or the loss of a loved one. Hopefully, the stories of survivors will not only inspire others to live their lives to the fullest, but also increase awareness of the pain and suffering inflicted by acts of terrorism.

GLOSSARY

civilians People who are not members of the military of a nation.

conscious To be awake and aware of oneself.

debris The remains of something that has been destroyed.

dictator One who rules absolutely and often oppressively.

evacuated To be taken or asked to move from a place, often in an emergency.

explosive A weapon that can be ignited and blown up.

extremists Individuals with radical views, some of whom commit murder or other acts of terrorism in support of their cause.

fatwa A declaration of war.

hijack To take a vehicle, often a plane, by force.

hostage Someone taken or detained by force or the threat of violence to secure the taker's demands.

medic A person professionally trained to treat injuries and sickness.

physical therapy Exercises and training to regain the use of weak or injured parts of the body.

prosthetic A device used to replace a missing body part.

suicide The act of taking one's own life.

terrorism The use of fear, by means of shooting, bombing, hijacking, etc., for political gain or to express political or religious displeasure.

FOR MORE INFORMATION

Center for Defense Information
1779 Massachusetts Avenue NW
Washington, DC 20036-2109
(202) 332-0600
E-mail: info@cdi.org
Web site: http://www.cdi.org

Federal Emergency Management Agency (FEMA)
500 C Street SW
Washington, DC 20472
(800) 621-FEMA (3362)
E-mail: FEMA-Correspondence-Unit@dhs.gov
Web site: http://www.fema.gov

The Institute for Counter-Terrorism
P.O. Box 167
Herzlia 46150
Israel
E-mail: info@ict.org.il
Web site: http://www.ict.org.il

U.S. Department of Homeland Security
Washington, DC 20528
(202) 282-8000
Web site : http://www.dhs.gov

World Trade Center Survivors' Network
22 Cortland Street, 20th Floor
New York, NY 10007
E-mail: contact@survivorsnet.org
Web site: http://www.survivorsnet.org

WEB SITES

Due to the changing nature of Internet links, Rosen Publishing has developed an online list of Web sites related to the subject of this book. This site is updated regularly. Please use this link to access the list:

http://www.rosenlinks.com/ss/terr

FOR FURTHER READING

Baker, David. *Suicide Bombers.* Vero Beach, FL: Rourke Publishing, 2005.

Casil, Amy Sterling. *Coping with Terrorism.* New York, NY: The Rosen Publishing Group, 2004.

Melter, Milton. *The Day the Sky Fell: A History of Terrorism.* New York, NY: Random House Books for Young Readers, 2002.

Moghadam, Assaf. *Roots of Terrorism.* New York, NY: Chelsea House Publishers, 2006.

Outman, James L., and Elisabeth M. Outman. *Terrorism Reference Library.* New York, NY: UXL, 2002.

Paul, Michael. *Oklahoma City and Anti-Government Terrorism.* Milwaukee, WI: World Almanac Library, 2006

Stewart, Gail. *America Under Attack: September 11, 2001.* San Diego, CA: Lucent Books, 2002.

Uschan, Michael V. *The Beslan School Siege and Separatist Terrorism.* Milwaukee, WI: Gareth Stevens Publishing, 2005.

BIBLIOGRAPHY

Barrett, Stephen. "'Priority One.'" BBC. November 2005. Retrieved
  April 2006 (http://news.bbc.co.uk/go/pr/fr/-/1/hi/magazine/
  4435172.stm).

BBC. "Beslan Boy Recalls Hostage Horror." Retrieved April 2006
  (http://news.bbc.co.uk/1/hi/world/europe/3641388.stm).

BBC. "Bomb Amputee Walks Down the Aisle." December 2005.
  Retrieved April 2006 (http://news.bbc.co.uk/go/pr/fr/-/1/hi/
  england/london/4515370.stm).

BBC. "Madrid Attacks Timeline." March 2004. Retrieved April 2006
  (http://news.bbc.co.uk/1/hi/world/europe/3504912.stm).

BBC. "Madrid Relives Horror of Attacks." 2005. Retrieved April 2006
  (http://news.bbc.co.uk/2/hi/europe/4335381.stm).

BBC. "Omagh Survivors Battle the Odds." 1999. Retrieved April
  2006 (http://news.bbc.co.uk/1/hi/special_report/regions/
  northern_ireland/419502.stm).

BBC. "On This Day." August 1998. Retrieved April 2006
  (http://news.bbc.co.uk/onthisday/hi/witness/august/15/newsid_
  3151000/3151015.stm).

BBC. "Reliving the London Bombing Horror." 2005. Retrieved April
  2006 (http://news.bbc.co.uk/go/pr/fr/-/1/hi/uk/4346812.stm).

Cassini, Dominic. "Living with the Omagh Legacy." 2002. Retrieved April 2006 (http://news.bbc.co.uk/1/hi/northern_ireland/ 1776332.stm).

CBS News. "School Siege Survivor's Tale." September 2004. Retrieved April 2006 (http://www.cbsnews.com/stories/2004/ 09/15/world/main643540.shtml).

Cheney, Peter. "'Teflon Man' Moves on and Finds New Joys in Life." *The Globe and Mail.* 2005. Retrieved April 2006 (http://www. theglobeandmail.com/special/attack/cheney/survivor05.html).

CNN. "Bombing Victim Lost Family, Leg." April 1996. Retrieved April 2006 (http://www.cnn.com/US/OKC/daily/9604/04-17/one_ year_later/daina.bradley/).

Dorsey, Jack. "*Cole* Survivors Think About, but Don't Dwell on, the Bombing." *Virginian Pilot.* 2005. Retrieved April 2006 (http:// home.hamptonroads.com/stories/story.cfm?story=93536& ran=107122).

Hamilton, Arnold. "Life Goes on for Young Survivors of Oklahoma City Bombing." Seattle Times. April 19, 2005. Retrieved April 2006 (http://seattletimes.nwsource.com/cgi-bin/PrintStory.pl? document_).

Larson, John. "Lesson from the Madrid Bombing." MSNBC. June 2005. Retrieved April 2006 (http://www.msnbc.msn.com/id/ 8074421/page/2/).

Luo, Michael. "The 91st Floor, Line Between Life and Death, Still Indelible." *New York Times.* September 2003. Retrieved April 2006 (http://www.911ea.org/News_Stories_From_September_2003.htm)

New York Times. "Fighting to Live as the Towers Died." May 26, 2002. Retrieved April 2006 (http://www.nytimes.com/2002/05/26/nyregion/26WTC.html?ex=1143781200&en=08637407c3c544a0&ei=5070).

9-11 Elisha Zion Peace Foundation. 2004. Retrieved April 2006 (http://www.headinjury.com/911ezpeace.htm).

PBS. "Above the Impact: A Survivor's Story." Retrieved April 2006 (http://www.pbs.org/wgbh/nova/wtc/above.html).

Petty, Linda. "USS *Cole* Survivor Recalls Aftermath of the Explosion." CNN. October 2000. Retrieved April 2006 (http://transcripts.cnn.com/2000/US/10/16/uss.cole.injured/).

Roberts, Adam. "The Changing Faces of Terrorism." BBC. 2004. Retrieved April 2006 (http://www.bbc.co.uk/history/war/sept_11/changing_faces_04.shtml)

Schulte, Bret. "Moving on, Looking Back." *U.S. News & World Report.* April 18, 2005. Retrieved April 2006 (http://www.usnews.com/usnews/news/articles/050418/18oklahoma.htm).

Tuchman, Gary. "Survivor Believes She Got a Second Chance." CNN. August 5, 1995. Retrieved April 2006 (http://www.cnn.com/US/OKC/faces/Survivors/Salyers8-5/index.html).

INDEX

ABOUT THE AUTHOR

Jennifer Silate is a writer and editor living and working in Annapolis, Maryland. She has written more than 100 books for children of all ages.

PHOTO CREDITS

Cover © Doug Kanter/AFP/Getty Images; p. 4 © Scott Peterson/Getty Images; pp. 9, 13, 15, 22, 26, 29, 39 © AP/Wide World Photos; p. 11 © Zuma Press/Newscom; p. 17 © Peter C. Brandt/Getty Images; p. 18 Courtesy Claire McIntyre; p. 24 © US Navy/Getty Images; p. 24 (inset) © Jim Watson/US Navy/Newsmakers/Getty Images; p. 32 © APTV/AP/Wide World Photos; p. 36 © Nadav Neuhaus/WpN.

Designer: Tahara Anderson; Editor: Wayne Anderson
Photo Researcher: Amy Feinberg